Lettice

Favourite Stories

The Dancing Rabbit
The Bridesmaid
The Fairy Ball

Mandy Stanley

HarperCollins *Children's Books*

Lettice

The Dancing Rabbit

Lettice Rabbit and her family lived high up on the top of the hill. Nibble, nibble, hop, hop, every day was the same…

until the day Lettice saw a picture pinned to a tree. It was then she knew that she wanted to be like the little girl in the picture. She wanted to be a dancer more than anything else in the world.

Lettice thought Town would be the best place to find out more, so she hopped there all by herself. She'd never been so far in her life.

Town was exciting – almost too exciting. There were lots of busy people, noisy babies, chatty children and big scary dogs!

Seeing an open door Lettice peeped in – and
there she saw dancers just like in the picture.
'I want to dance!' she cried rushing in.
The music stopped and everybody looked.
'Please may I join in?' asked Lettice shyly.
'Yes,' said the surprised teacher, 'but first
you must get dressed in ballet clothes.'

Lettice didn't know what to do – she had never worn clothes before.

'You can get them at the shop we get ours from,' called out a little girl.

At the shop Lettice tried on all the clothes,

but the dress dragged
on the floor,

the shoes were
like flippers,

and the cardigan
was huge.

Lettice began
to cry.

Then the shop assistant
brought out a ballerina doll.

All the doll's clothes
fitted perfectly.

Now Lettice was ready!

Lettice hopped back to the ballet class.
    First, she had to learn the ballet positions.
She watched and listened very carefully
copying the other dancers. The ballet
teacher showed her how to hold her head
high so her ears would look graceful.

Lettice worked very hard.

She turned out
her long toes,

she stretched up her arms

and she tried not to wobble. When she jumped...

it looked as though she were flying! When she

twirled and whirled she was almost a blur.

Every week, Lettice went to Town for her class and at home she practised every spare minute of the day.

The teacher thought Lettice was very special and was amazed at her extraordinary jumps.

Lettice worked so hard that each night she went to bed very tired – but happy.

A few weeks later it was the end of term show.
Lettice had been chosen for the starring role.
She had a gorgeous costume – there was
even a tiny crown!

All Lettice's family had come to see her.
Lettice was so nervous she thought she'd
never be able to dance at all!

Lettice Rabbit and her family lived high up on top of the hill. Nibble, nibble, hop, hop, every day was the same but one day...

Lettice popped her head out of the burrow
and saw a letter fluttering on a bush.
'It's for ME!' she squeaked.

Later, Giselle had presents for Lettice and Harry.
'I want to thank you both for helping to make this
the happiest day of my life,' she said.

'And I have a
present for you,'
said Lettice.

She twirled and
whirled...

..and spun around in
vn special dance,
for Giselle.

The moon was up by the time Lettice and her family set off home. Lettice was so tired that her father had to carry her to their burrow.

'It's been a perfect day,' she whispered
sleepily. 'The most perfect day of my life.'

Lettice

The Fairy Ball

Lettice Rabbit and her family lived high up on top of a hill. Nibble, nibble, hop, hop, every day was the same, until one summer afternoon...

Lettice was making daisy chains
when she felt a sharp tug…

The daisy chain
s-t-r-e-t-c-h-e-d and,
ping, it broke and
whisked away.

Two tiny figures with
shimmering wings were
pulling it through the air.
'Stop!' shrieked Lettice.

All of a sudden, they
swooped down a hole in the
roots of an old oak.

Lettice pressed her
nose inside but she was too
big to go through. 'Who *are* you?'
she cried. 'What are you *doing*?'

Lettice jumped back. Suddenly, in front of her, was a group of tiny people. 'Rabbit,' laughed one, 'our Queen needs your daisy chain for the Fairy Ball in Fairyland.'

'Fairyland?' squeaked Lettice.
'I'd like to go to Fairyland.
But I'm too big!'

'If you give us your chain, we will sprinkle fairy dust on you,' giggled a chorus of little voices, and the air filled with golden sparkles.

'Atishoo!'
sneezed Lettice.
Suddenly, she was
shrinking...

and shrinking...

and then she was
no bigger than an oak leaf!

Happily, Lettice
dashed into the hole
after the fairies.

Inside, it was dark, but soon
she came to a door and
through it was...

FAIRYLAND!

'Quickly, now,' said the fairies, 'it's time to put on our best clothes to welcome the Queen.'

Lettice's face fell.
What was she going
to wear?

'Don't worry,' laughed
the fairies. 'Just
close your eyes!'
Lettice stood still.

She could feel
something soft and
light, smelling of
flowers, dropping
over her ears.

It was the
prettiest little
fairy dress,
trimmed with
thistledown.

Just then, a bossy elf cried,
'Make way for Her Majesty, Queen Titania!'
The Fairy Queen had arrived!

She was riding in a carriage made of yellow
rose petals, drawn by a yellow bird, and
her reins were... Lettice's daisy chain!

'Welcome, little rabbit. Thank you for my
beautiful reins,' smiled the Queen, holding out
a tiny bracelet. 'This is for you. It will grant you
one wish – use it well.'

Then young elves brought out the most wonderful fairy feast.

Afterwards, everyone danced
– especially Lettice!

All too soon it was time to go.
'We won't forget you, Lettice,'
called the fairies, waving goodbye.
'Wait!' squeaked Lettice. 'I'm still small!'

Just then, a cloud of
fairy dust floated
down, making Lettice's
nose twitch.

The ground felt all
wobbly and she was
growing bigger...

and bigger...

and bigger, until
she was the right size.

In two hops and a jump,
Lettice was home. She
bounced in to tell her family
all about the fairies.

'They're ever so small and pretty,' she sighed.
'Oh, I *wish* you could see them, too.'

Just then, the magic bracelet on her paw glowed and Lettice was sure she heard fairy laughter.

Lettice's brothers and sisters couldn't believe their eyes! Fluttering above them were hundreds of smiling fairies.

As she gazed up, Lettice murmured happily,
'My wish came true! I'm such a lucky rabbit.'

First published in hardback in Great Britain by HarperCollins Children's Books in 2010
First published as *Lettice – The Dancing Rabbit* in 2001, *Lettice – The Bridesmaid* in 2005 and *Lettice – The Fairy Ball* in 2006

1 3 5 7 9 10 8 6 4 2

ISBN: 978-0-00-787950-2

HarperCollins Children's Books is a division of HarperCollins Publishers Ltd.

Visit our website at: www.harpercollins.co.uk

Printed and bound in China